FEAR

Jonny Zucker

Illustrated by Tom Percival

Ginn

Chapter 1

Rick Walker was flash. He sported designer gear. He wore a silvery-blue ring on his middle finger. And he was gadget-crazy. You could count on him to get his hands on the latest gizmos before anyone else.

On the first day of the autumn term, he arrived in school with a new mobile phone – the just-released Zed 5. He was showing it off to some mates in the corridor outside his classroom. It was the smallest phone anyone had ever seen, with a gleaming silver casing and a dark orange screen. The keys were stylish purple rectangles. The Zed 5 logo shone out from the centre of the phone and there were a few gasps of awe as people stared at it.

"Its battery life is twice as long as any other phone," Rick boasted, "and it's totally damage-proof."

He threw the phone onto the floor and bent down to pick it up. "See," he exclaimed, holding it up to the gathered crowd, "It's unbreakable."

"Give us a go," shouted several people and Rick passed it round, letting some of his classmates try it out. A few took photos with it. Someone sent a speed text message. A boy called Steve even made a quick call. When Steve finished with the phone, he pulled a face at Rick. "I was only on it for a few seconds," Steve said, "but my ear really hurts."

Rick snatched the Zed 5 back out of Steve's hand. "Don't be stupid," he told Steve, "your ear's fine."

Steve rubbed his ear and shook his head. "Seriously, it feels like someone's given my ear an electric shock."

Rick put his hand on Steve's shoulder. "You've always had a good imagination," he said smiling.

"No – Steve's right!" said a boy, standing a few metres away from the others. Everyone turned round. It was Taz Singh – the class technology genius. People who'd been round to Taz's house said his bedroom was a jumble of electrical leads and wires, and was filled with half-built computers and old radios.

"Last week I saw a programme on TV about the new generation of mobiles," Taz continued. "It claimed they could be really dangerous. It mentioned a few types of mobiles and one of them was the Zed 5."

There was silence for a moment and then Rick burst out laughing.

"You spend too much time in your bedroom with your old toasters or whatever it is you've got in there. Chill out and stop watching boring TV programmes. There are always people going on about how bad mobiles are for you, but can you see anyone round here sprouting two heads?"

A few of the other kids laughed. But Taz stood his ground. "I'm not joking, Rick. A guy on the programme warned people to treat the Zed 5 with extreme caution. Your new phone might cause you some big trouble."

Helen Parsons had been quiet so far, but now she nodded seriously. She was Rick's best friend, but she also got on well with Taz.

"Maybe Taz has a point," she said, looking at Rick. "We don't really know that much about mobiles."

"You're right, Helen."

It was their teacher, Mrs Dean. She was standing in the doorway of their classroom, and had just overheard their conversation.

"None of you are ill now. But what about in thirty or forty years? Maybe we'll all be paying the price for mobile technology in the future," Mrs Dean added.

Everyone was silent for a moment. Even Rick.

"Anyway," Mrs Dean continued, "you'll be delighted to know it's Maths, so come into class quietly and settle down."

All of the children groaned and shuffled into the classroom.

Rick walked to his table and scowled back at Taz. "Loser," he mouthed.

Chapter 2

That night at home, Rick sat in the living room holding his Zed 5 and trying out all of its functions.

He'd skipped all of the boring bits in the User Manual. There was a page about 'Phone Safety' but he ignored it, grinning to himself for a second about Taz's warnings. That guy lived in a different world.

So far, Rick had used his Zed 5 to watch some real-time video clips of a football match, log on to a couple of surfing websites and customise his ring tone to blare out his favourite band's latest single.

"Dinner's ready!" his dad called from the kitchen doorway.

Rick didn't look up from the phone's screen. He was testing out the digital camera menu and was marvelling at the incredible quality of the pictures the phone took.

The camera was miles better than anyone else's in school. And because the Zed 5 was pretty expensive, he was sure it would be a long time before any of his mates could afford one.

"Didn't you hear me?" complained his dad, walking into the room. "Your food's hot and I'm not going to reheat it."

He looked down at the Zed 5 in Rick's hand. "I can see you're thrilled to bits with your new phone, but I'm not going to let it take over your life. And I know you've saved up for that phone, but that doesn't mean you can spend every waking second with it. Now put it away and come and eat with us."

Rick remained fixated by the movements on the screen.

"NOW!" snapped his dad, "or I'll take it away from you."

Rick sighed, flipped the phone shut and slipped it into his pocket.

His mum was waiting in the kitchen, reading a newspaper. She raised her eyes to the heavens when Rick walked in. He could tell she'd had a bad day at work. She looked tired and hassled.

"At least we haven't completely lost you," she sighed. "Sometimes I wish we'd never said 'Yes' to you having a mobile. They just interfere with everyone's lives. When I was young ..."

"Yeah, yeah, Mum," Rick groaned, looking bored. "When you were young the only way of contacting your mates was to send a letter by horseback."

"Enough of that cheek," she replied. "Now eat your dinner or I'll confiscate that phone."

Rick felt the Zed 5 in his pocket. There was no way he could allow his parents to take it away from him.

Later in his room, Rick glanced at the pile of homework waiting for his attention. It would take him hours to get all of it done. Why did Mrs Dean insist on giving them so much? Wasn't she a kid once? He picked up the pile of worksheets, dropped them into his desk drawer and slammed the drawer shut. He'd do it before school tomorrow. There were far more important matters to deal with first.

It was nearly midnight when Rick finally switched off his new phone. His parents had poked their heads round his door at ten o'clock and had told him to turn out his light. When they'd looked in, Rick was lying on his bed with a book placed in front of the Zed 5. He seemed like the perfect student.

Rick had actually spent the whole evening texting friends to let them know that he was now the Mobile Phone King. He'd also tried out all of the games on the Zed 5. Now, Rick connected the phone to its charger and plugged the charger into the wall socket underneath his desk. The fluorescent dark blue steps on the screen began to rise, indicating that the phone was being charged.

As Rick climbed into bed, he thought briefly about Steve's complaint that the Zed 5 had hurt his ear. Rick smiled to himself. He'd made several whispered calls that evening and his ear was absolutely fine. Steve didn't know what he was talking about.

Giving the phone one final glance, he shut his eyes and fell asleep quickly. His dreams were filled with huge text messages and

figures from space games.

In the early hours of the morning, Rick's dreams were interrupted. He woke up coughing and spluttering. His throat felt parched and scratchy. It took his eyes a second to adjust to the light, but as soon as he focused, he saw a thick haze of purplish smoke drifting across the room. There was a weird burning smell in the air.

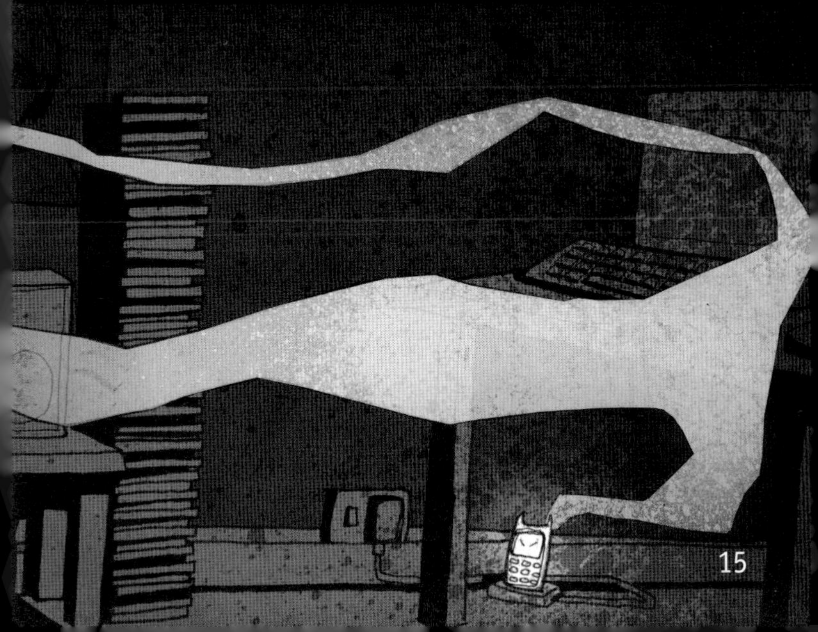

He coughed again and jumped out of bed. What was happening? He needed to get to his parents' room to tell them there was a fire, and to call a fire engine. But, as he coughed his way towards the door, he suddenly saw where the smoke was coming from. It was flowing out of his Zed 5, which lay where he'd left it under his desk.

The smoke smelt strongly and Rick suddenly felt overpowered by the fumes, as they spiralled down his throat and into his lungs. He waved his arms wildly in the air, trying to steer the smoke away from his face. Panicking, he lurched across the room, feeling as if some unseen hand was choking him.

He was about to open his bedroom door when a thought struck him. If he woke his mum and dad, and they saw where the smoke was coming from, they'd confiscate the Zed 5 immediately. No, he had to sort this out himself.

Rick crossed the room and frantically yanked the charger out of the socket. Then he moved quickly to the other side of his room to fling open the window. He leant his head out and felt relief as the cool breeze drew the smoke into the night air. He reached for a glass of water on his shelf and took a long drink. His throat ached and his lungs throbbed with pain.

The smoke gradually drifted out of the window. He sat down on his bed, and rubbed his throat gingerly. He coughed again. The acrid smell still hung in the air. He watched the last wisps of smoke curl up and out of his window.

When all the smoke had cleared, Rick stepped over to his desk. He knelt down to pick up the Zed 5. As soon as his hand came into contact with the phone's casing, he yelped in pain and dropped it back onto the floor. It was like touching fire. The Zed 5 was white-hot.

Rick blew on his hand and stared at the phone. He knew charging phones could heat up a bit, but surely not like that? This one was burning hot. If he hadn't woken up, there might have been a massive fire. He checked his hand. There were no marks on it, but it still felt a bit sore.

Rick sat in the chair in front of his desk, staring at the Zed 5. There was no smoke coming out of it anymore. The screen showed that it was fully charged.

He rooted around on his desk and found the phone's User Manual. He thumbed through the pages until he got to the 'Troubleshooting' section. On the page about charging there was a line about overheating. It said that the Zed 5, if left on a charger for too long, could overheat. Rick sighed with relief. It didn't say anything about producing smoke, but he'd read enough to calm himself down a bit. Maybe all Zed Fives did this when they were charged for the first time.

Or maybe it had been something completely different. Perhaps it had been a power surge that set the mobile off. There was a lot of electricity sparking around any house. Maybe it was that. He couldn't remember the last time an electrician had been in the house to check anything out. There could be old or faulty wiring anywhere.

Rick decided that the next time he charged the Zed 5, he'd use another electrical socket.

It could be that the one under his desk was faulty. He cautiously leant out and touched the Zed 5 with one of his fingertips. It was cool now. He picked it up, put it on top of his desk and got back into bed.

As he lay down, he realised that he was shaking. *Relax*, he told himself, *there's nothing to freak out about. If you worry about the phone, you'll end up sounding like Taz. So it got a bit hot. Big deal. There's absolutely nothing wrong with the phone.*

He turned to the wall and tried not to think about the phone. But his throat felt sore and he could still smell smoke in his nostrils. He tossed and turned for a while, thinking about the purplish smoke that had come from his new mobile.

He finally went back to sleep.

Chapter 3

Rick had no trouble with the Zed 5 for the rest of the week. He charged it again, but this time he did it when he was awake, and he used a socket near his bedside table. It took a couple of hours to charge, and he stayed in the room with it the whole time. If it billowed out smoke again, he needed to be there to get to it before either of his parents noticed anything was up. But it charged without any problems and when Rick gingerly touched it to pull it out of the socket, it felt cool to the touch. He grinned to himself and flicked to one of the space games on the phone.

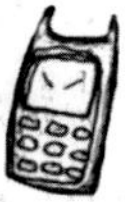

On Friday night, Rick went over to Helen's house to watch a DVD with her and some of their friends. He thought about mentioning the overheating Zed 5 incident, but decided against it. She was a good mate, but sometimes she behaved like an extra parent.

"You took your time!" Helen mocked as she opened the front door to Rick.

"I had to make a couple of calls on the way," he grinned, nodding 'Hellos' to everyone else.

"I asked Taz to come too, but he couldn't make it," Helen said.

"You're joking, aren't you?" Rick asked with surprise. "Why did you ask that weirdo?"

"Give him a break," replied Helen.

"Whatever," scoffed Rick.

"Anyway," she continued, "when I asked him to come over, he sounded really anxious about something. I've never heard him going on like that. Sounded like he was completely freaking out. I'm a bit worried about him."

Rick laughed. "He's probably slipped himself into one of his computer drives and can't find the eject button."

A couple of the others laughed at this and Rick reached into his jacket pocket to pull out his Zed 5. There were a few people here who hadn't seen his new toy yet, and he wasn't going to miss an opportunity to show it off.

Helen stared at the phone, frowned and moved closer towards Rick.

"What's up?" Rick asked.

"What happened to your hand?" asked Helen.

"What do you mean?" he said, following her gaze.

He looked down and saw that the fingers on his left hand were badly bruised. They looked really bad. They were covered in large patches of black and blue.

"You haven't been in a fight, have you?" asked Helen.

Rick shook his head, unable to speak. How could he have picked up such bad bruises without noticing? To mark your hand like that you needed to smash your fingers against a wall, or have them crushed by a brick. His mind suddenly flashed back to the incident with the phone-charging, and he felt his heart beat quickening.

Rick had decided that he wasn't going to tell Helen about the phone overheating, but he instantly changed his mind. His voice dropped to a whisper, because he didn't want any of the others to know. They might laugh at him and say the Zed 5 was dangerous.

He quickly described the smoke in his bedroom and the searing heat of the Zed 5. As he was telling Helen about this, he kept looking down at his bruised fingers and wondering how they'd ended up like that.

As he talked, Helen gazed at Rick with shock. She looked from Rick's face to his fingers again. "That's the hand you use to make calls on, isn't it?" she asked.

He checked the bruises again and nodded nervously.

"I don't like it," Helen muttered. "I bet the phone did that to your hand."

"Don't be ridiculous," Rick hissed. "A phone couldn't do that!"

Helen eyed him seriously. "Well how did it happen then?" she asked. "It just seems like too much of a coincidence to me."

Rick was silent for a moment, a whirl of thoughts flashing through his mind. *Surely the Zed 5 couldn't have done this?*

Helen hadn't finished. "It sounds like something's seriously wrong with that phone, Rick. Even if it didn't hurt your hand, the overheating thing sounds wrong. Have you checked the instruction booklet?"

"Of course I have," protested Rick. He sensed Helen was about to give him a lecture. "It didn't mention anything like this."

"Well there's only one thing to do then," said Helen firmly. "Take it back."

Rick's first thought was to argue with her, but as he moved his fingers tighter around the Zed 5, they ached a bit. "Okay," he nodded. "I'll do it tomorrow."

Chapter 4

The following afternoon, Rick was in town with his mum. They'd been looking for some new trainers, but the ones he really wanted hadn't reached the shops yet. His mum had tried to persuade Rick to go for some others, but he didn't budge. Once he'd made his mind up about something, he rarely changed it.

Now they stood outside a large department store.

"I've got to go to the mobile phone shop," Rick announced, keeping his bruised hand in his pocket. He'd been extra careful to not let his parents see it. They'd only ask lots of questions and make a fuss.

"What for?" she asked. "You've only just got that new phone."

"It's for a case," he replied quickly. "It won't cost much."

"Fine," she said, "I'll come with you."

Rick shook his head. "No, I'll be okay on my own. I'll meet you under the clock tower in an hour."

His mum sighed. "Fine, but don't be late."

Rick watched her walk off and vanish into the crowd. He turned and headed for the phone shop. The queue wasn't as big as he'd anticipated and he found himself at the service desk pretty quickly, facing a familiar-looking, smartly dressed woman.

"The boy who bought the Zed 5," she smiled. She'd served Rick when he'd made his purchase a week ago.

Rick nodded and quickly told her about the smoke incident and then showed her his bruised fingers. She listened carefully to his story and frowned.

"Obviously it's early days for the Zed 5," she said, "and because of their high price, we only managed to get a few delivered to this store. The manager bought one – he's off sick today, so I can't ask him about it. One was recalled to the factory – there was something wrong with the Sim card. And you bought the other one. So I haven't really heard anything about this model. But I'll phone our head office straight away and check to see if there have been any similar incidents reported."

She dialled a number, then stood drumming her fingers on the counter as she waited for an answer. After a few minutes she shook her head. "No one's answering at the moment," she said, "but I'll speak to them later and get back to you if there have been any other cases like this. Why don't you leave your Zed 5 here for the time being? I'll get you a replacement phone while I look into it. Just pick any model you like."

Rick quickly shook his head. However much the Zed 5 had freaked him out, there was no way he was going to hand it over and go back to using some crummy old phone. "It's okay. I'll hang onto it," he replied.

"That's fine," she replied, "but as I said – if I hear anything, then I'll call you. In the meantime, maybe you shouldn't use the phone."

Rick shrugged his shoulders and left the shop.

When Rick and his mum returned home, his dad told him that Helen had phoned and that she wanted him to call her back.

Rick went up to his bedroom and made the call.

"What happened with your mobile?" Helen asked.

"It's all okay," Rick replied. "It's nothing. They're going to look into it, but the woman in the shop hadn't had any other complaints. She said she'd phone if there had been any."

"Well, if you say so," replied Helen, sounding unsure. "But I think you're stupid to keep on using it. You can live without it for a few days, can't you? Especially if there's something wrong with it."

"I said there's nothing wrong with it!" snapped Rick, beginning to lose his temper.

"All right, calm down," said Helen. "Oh, and by the way, Taz has called me several times today. He says he needs to talk to you urgently."

Rick groaned. *Why did it feel like everyone was on his case?* "What programme has he been watching now?" Rick asked. "Taz needs to take it easy and get away from his electro-junk for a while."

"He sounded very serious," Helen said. "I really think you should call him."

"No way!" scoffed Rick. "I don't want to listen to any of his rubbish. My phone's fine. End of story. Let him go and bother someone else."

Chapter 5

At the end of school on Monday, Mrs Dean kept Rick back to ask him where his missing homework was. He made a feeble excuse about losing it, and only managed to get away from her by promising he'd have it all ready first thing the next morning.

He hurried to the cloakroom. He'd left his bag there by accident during an afternoon break. The bag was exactly where he'd left it and he opened it to check everything was inside. His pen and schoolbooks were all there, but there was no sign of the Zed 5. He quickly searched his bag again, but without any joy.

Rick cursed under his breath. Someone must have nicked it. The thought of going home to tell his parents that he'd lost his brand new phone was giving him a complete nightmare.

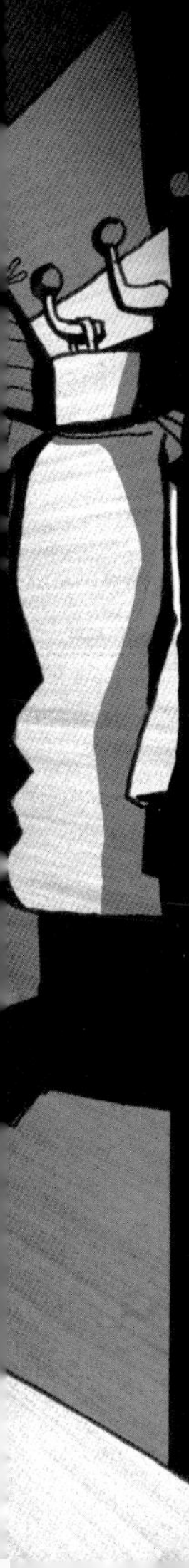

Just as he was hitting the wall furiously, he heard his name being called. It was Helen.

"I've got your phone, Rick," she called. "My mobile ran out and I needed to call my mum to tell her I'm staying for a choir practice. I saw you talking to Mrs Dean, so I reckoned you wouldn't mind if I borrowed yours."

Rick sighed with relief. Then he noticed Helen's face.

"What's up?" Helen asked.

Helen's right eye looked really bloodshot.

There was a thin reddish-purple ring around her whole eye. She looked like some creature from a badly-made sci-fi film. Her eye had looked fine when he last saw her, five minutes ago. In the meantime, the only thing she'd done was use his Zed 5.

He felt the muscles in his stomach tighten.

"It's your ... your ..."

But Rick didn't get to finish his sentence. Helen chucked him the phone and spun off in the direction of the music room.

"Gotta go!" she called. "Don't want to be late."

Rick watched her hurry off down the corridor. Then he turned and began to run as fast as he could.

Chapter 6

Rick sat on the park bench, shaking. He'd been sitting there for ages, just staring down at the Zed 5 inside his school bag. He'd thought about just tossing the phone into a dustbin, but then he'd had a vision of someone finding it and being seriously injured. The police would be sure to trace the phone back to him and then he'd be in big trouble.

He suddenly remembered Helen's bloodshot eye. He was sure the phone, his phone, had caused it. But he didn't have time to worry about her – he had his image to think about. He'd talked about nothing else since he'd bought the Zed 5. What would the other kids in school say when he turned up without it? And if he told them the truth, they'd probably just laugh at him.

Rick had been in the park for over an hour when he finally decided what he was going to do. He had to go and see Taz. As much as he hated to admit it, Taz was the only person who could help him now. He'd phone Helen, get Taz's address and go there straight away. Before he changed his mind.

Rick pounded down the High Street, past the chemists' and over the zebra crossing, and then stopped to get his breath back. There was no way he was going to use his Zed 5 to call Helen. There were three phone boxes further down the High Street outside *Pizza Please*. He ran on to them.

The first one had been vandalised and was covered in graffiti. Rick swore to himself. He ran into the second one and picked up the receiver.

"Sorry," announced a metallic voice, "there is a fault on this line. Sorry, there is a fault on this line ..."

He slammed the phone down and headed for the third phone box.

There was a young woman inside the last phone box, talking very slowly. Rick saw she had placed a large pile of coins on top of the phone unit. He waited impatiently for a few seconds, and then knocked on the glass. This couldn't wait. The woman turned round to face him. She eyed him coldly.

"Emergency," he mouthed, pointing towards the receiver in her hand. She scowled at him and returned to her conversation.

He pulled open the door and shouted, "Get out of here! I need to make a call now!"

The woman eyed him with contempt, said goodbye to the other person, and picked up her pile of coins. She stamped out of the phone box, muttering something about 'rude children nowadays'.

Rick fumbled for change in his pocket and slipped a coin into the pay phone. A rattling noise sounded as the coin toppled into the change tray.

999 calls only read the display.

Rick hit the phone with his fist. The woman he'd just kicked out had been talking normally. The phone *must* be working.

999 calls only flashed the display again.

Rick looked round and saw a small group of people outside the phone box looking at him warily. He pushed the door open and stamped out of the box, nudging a couple of people out of the way. He leant against the window of the hardware shop and tried to think clearly. But his thoughts kept coming back to the woman in the phone shop. *Why hadn't he left the phone with her like she had said?* Then he wouldn't be in this mess.

He checked his watch. He was already going to be very late getting home. His mum was very strict about letting her know where he was. Whenever he was late and didn't phone her, she went completely mad. He tried to push this thought out of his mind. She would kill him. But he didn't have time to phone her. He had to phone Helen. He had no choice. He needed Taz's help.

He reached into his bag and picked up the Zed 5 with fear. *Helen should be home from choir practice by now*, Rick thought to himself. He dialled Helen's home number with trembling hands. Then he pressed the 'loudspeaker' option and held the phone as far away from his ear as possible. After a couple of rings, Helen answered.

"Hello?"

"It's Rick. I need to know where Taz lives."

He knew he ought to ask how Helen's eye was, but he didn't.

"I can't really speak now, Rick. My mum wants to use the phone to call the doctor's. My eye is looking really weird! Did you not notice it?"

"Look, I'm in a hurry too. Can you give me Taz's address?" Rick's stomach turned over when he realised how serious things had become.

"Is this some kind of wind up?" laughed Helen. "Remember, you think he's a techno nerd."

"This isn't a joke, Helen. Where does Taz live? I need to know."

"Okay, okay," she replied. "He lives at number 50, Grange Road. But what do you want with him?"

Rick said nothing.

"It's something to do with that phone of yours, isn't it?" said Helen. "I knew it was bad news."

But before Rick could reply, he suddenly felt an agonising bolt of pain in his left cheek. It were as if half of his face had been pushed into a furnace. He dropped the Zed 5 on the ground as pain shot across his face. He grasped his cheek in agony and staggered forward, crashing into a lamp post. He crumpled in a heap outside the hardware shop. It was the worst pain he'd ever experienced and he had to fight to stop himself screaming out in desperation and terrifying half of the High Street.

He could hear Helen's voice calling out.

"Rick? Are you there? Rick, what's going on?" Suddenly, the Zed 5 bleeped to announce the call was over.

Rick managed to stand up and look in the shop window. There was his reflection looking back at him, with a grotesque red patch etched onto his cheek.

He looked down with revulsion at the Zed 5 on the floor. Things had gone too far now. The phone was out of control. It had a life of its own. It was evil.

Okay, he told himself, trying to calm down. *You've got Taz's address. Everything's going to be okay. Just get the phone to Taz.*

If he was going to pick the Zed 5 up, he needed some sort of protection. He reached down into his bag and pulled out his Maths book. Then he carefully scooped up the phone between two pages of the book and dropped it into his bag.

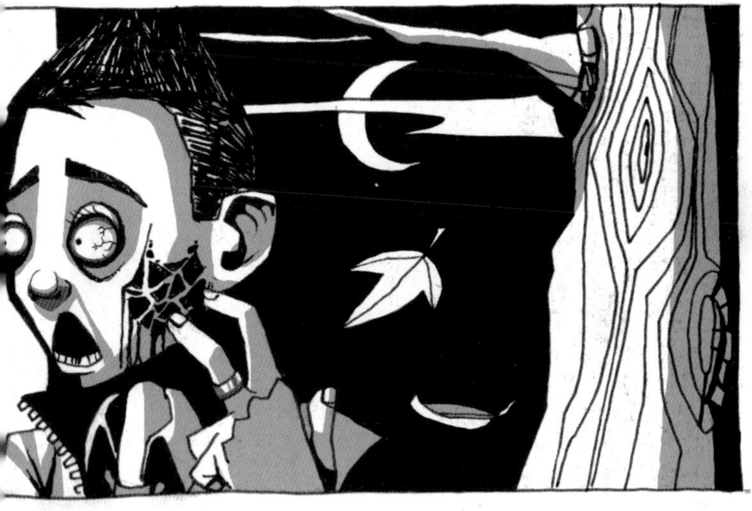

He ran into the newsagents and grabbed an ice lolly from the freezer cabinet. The man in the shop couldn't take his eyes off Rick's scarred cheek. Rick threw some coins onto the counter and ran back out into the street.

He ripped open the packet and held the cool ice against his burning cheek. He winced in pain. The ice was soothing, but the pain was still agonising.

As he stood there, his mind was tumbling over with terrifying thoughts. The purple smoke in his bedroom; the burning hot phone; the bruised fingers; Helen's eye; the red patch on his face. They were all connected. The Zed 5 should never have been sold in the shops. The people who'd made the Zed 5 either didn't know about its power. Or they didn't care.

Chapter 7

Rick reached the end of the High Street and turned into Grange Street. The first house on the even side of the road was number two. He gritted his teeth and ran on.

He pounded on the door of number fifty.

Taz eventually appeared. He looked at Rick's face with horror. "What's going on?" he asked.

"It's the phone," gasped Rick. "It's lethal."

"I've been trying to tell you that for ages," replied Taz.

"Okay," muttered Rick angrily, "you were right. I've said it. What more do you want?"

"I don't want anything," shrugged Taz.

"You've got to help me!" Rick pleaded. "How bad can this phone get?"

Taz sighed. "There have been loads of notices on different websites, about the dangers of the Zed 5. The company that makes them says there's nothing wrong with them. But some people swear they've had their fingers crushed and others say the phone has partially blinded them. If it's doing those sort of things, who knows what might happen next?"

Rick pulled the phone out of his bag from between the pages of his Maths book and held it out towards Taz. "Take it off me and destroy it," said Rick. "You're the only person I know who can do something about it."

Taz shrunk back. "No way!" he yelled. "Get that thing away from me. I'm not laying a finger on it."

"Well, what am I supposed to do?" shouted Rick. His whole body was shot through with nervous energy. "Someone's got to do something about it!"

Taz watched silently as Rick's anxiety poured out. "Okay. I'll tell you what you need to do," Taz said.

"Good," nodded Rick nervously, "but make it quick before something really serious happens."

"Okay," Taz said. "You know the recycling centre on the other side of the park?"

"Yeah."

"They have a section there that's just for mobile phones that have packed up. You're not supposed to throw mobiles away. They recondition them or dispose of them. That's the best thing I can think of. They have a couple of people there who know what they're doing. Take the Zed 5 to them and explain what's happened. They'll take it off you and destroy it safely."

"Are you sure?" Rick asked.

"Yeah," Taz replied, "go there straight away before it does any more damage. And whatever you do, don't touch it. Leave that up to them."

Rick dropped the Maths book and the Zed 5 back into his bag. He sprinted off down the street.

He didn't even bother to thank Taz.

Chapter 8

Rick ran faster than he'd ever done before. A couple of motorists and passers-by stopped to watch the speeding boy with the huge red mark on his face.

But Rick didn't pay attention to anyone else.

He cut through the shopping centre, nearly colliding with a security guard.

"Hey! Watch where you're going!" shouted the guard.

But Rick ignored him and everyone else. He pushed a group of window shoppers out of his path and came out through the revolving doors at the far end of the shopping centre. He didn't care about the trail of angry people he left behind. All he could think about was saving himself. The blood was pounding in his ears, but he knew he had to keep going. He had no choice.

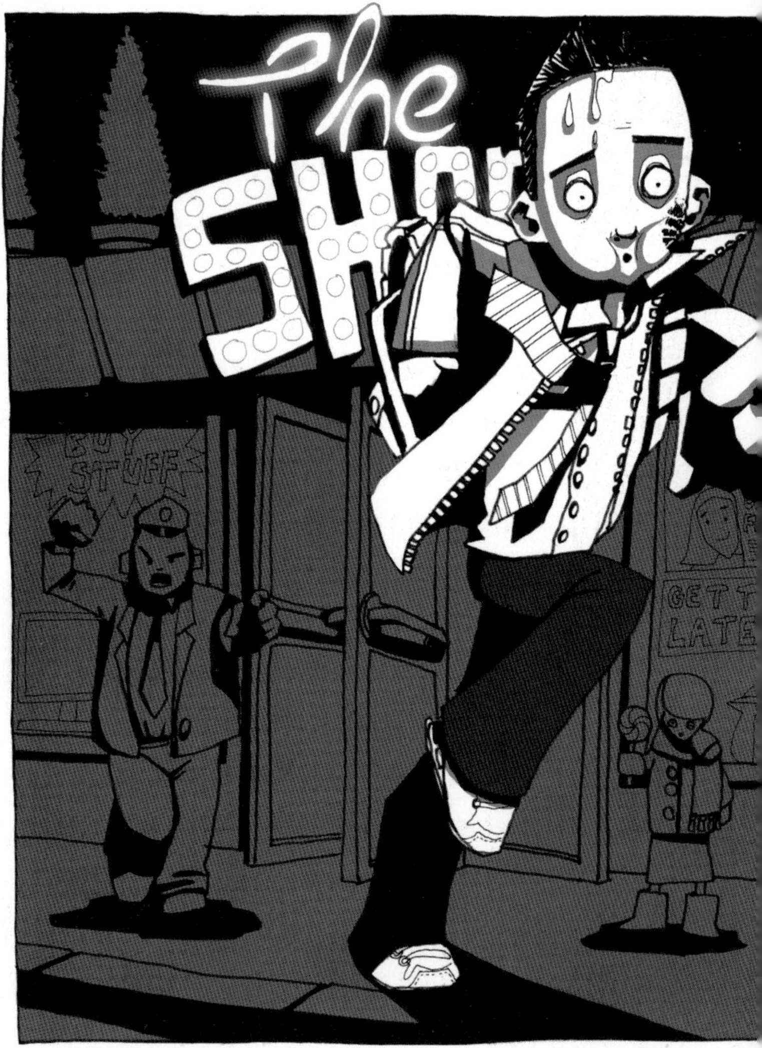
The
BUY STUFF

He sped down the street and, as he turned the corner, the park came into view. He was nearly at the first set of park gates, when the ring tone of his Zed 5 went. He crunched to a halt.

He glanced down into his bag and saw 'Mum' displayed on the Zed 5's screen. He chewed his bottom lip. It was an agonising choice. Taz had told him not to touch the phone, but he was now going to be an hour late getting home. His mum would be frantic with worry.

He thought back to the useless phone boxes on the High Street and made an instant decision. He'd take the call, but it would be the last time he would ever use the Zed 5.

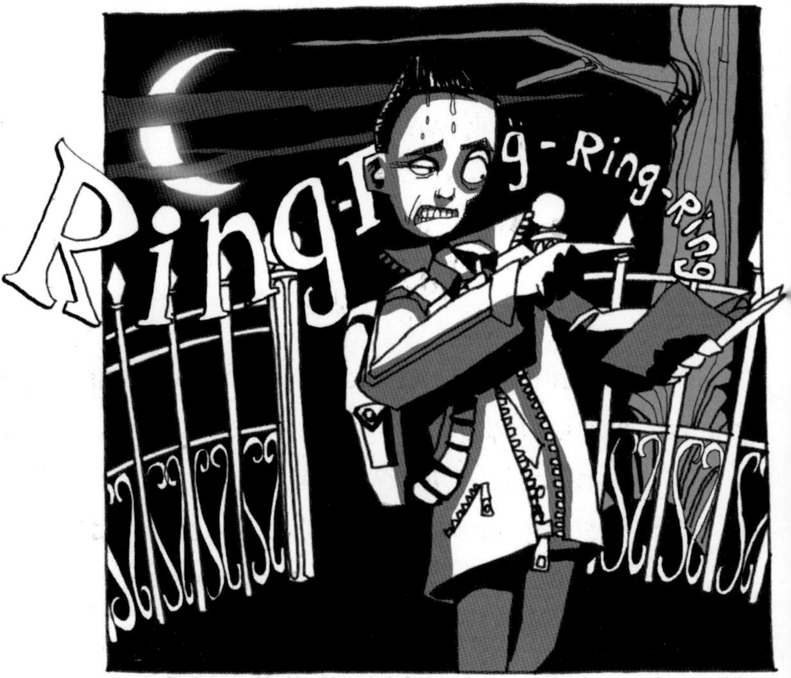

Rick lifted the phone up with the pages of his Maths book. He put one finger over the pages and pressed the 'answer' key.

"Where are you?" his mum asked.

"I'm nearly home," Rick lied. "I'm doing something."

"What sort of something?"

"I'm just outside the main park gates," he replied, "and I'm ..."

The line suddenly went dead.

Rick's mum heard the bleep, signalling that the call had ended.

"Rick!" she called. "Rick?"

She held the receiver in her hand, confused and worried. Rick had sounded upset and scared. That wasn't at all like her son. She tried his mobile number again, but got his voicemail.

"Rick. It's me again," she said. "What are you up to? If it's something to do with school, don't worry. Is it about homework again? If it is, it's not a big deal. Just come home and let's talk about it."

Rick's mum looked at a set of numbers posted on the fridge door and dialled Helen's number. She was relieved when Helen answered the call after just two rings.

"Helen, it's Joan, Rick's mum. I just had a really strange phone call with him. He sounded frightened. Then the phone cut off. Do you know what he's up to? Is he in some sort of trouble?"

"Do you know where he is?" asked Helen.

"He said he was outside the park gates. Why do you ask?"

"Oh, I'm sure it's nothing, Mrs Walker," Helen replied, "but I'll phone another friend just to check. I'll get back to you in a couple of minutes."

Helen dialled Taz's number frantically.

"Did Rick come and see you just now?" she demanded, when Taz answered.

"Yeah," Taz replied. "He was here about fifteen minutes ago, asking me how to get rid of his phone. He looked pretty bad – one of his cheeks was really red and sore."

"His mum has just rung me. He spoke to her on his mobile from outside the park gates, and then the line went dead. I think something really bad has happened to him."

Taz jumped off his chair and pulled on his jacket. "I'm on my way," he said.

Taz flew down the stairs, shouted 'Bye!' to his mum, and sped out of the front door. He grabbed his bike and pushed off down the street. He hurtled forward, hoping that Rick had made it to the recycling centre.

Taz pulled up in front of the park gates. He dismounted and pushed the bike against the railings. He scanned the street ahead, but there was no sign of Rick. Maybe everything was fine and he was already at the recycling centre, sorting things out? Taz walked back to his bike and was about to cycle off, when something on the ground caught his eye.

At the base of one of the park gates, under an overhanging branch, was Rick's silvery-blue ring.

Taz hurried over and knelt down beside the gate. He pulled the branch out of the way, and a shock of terror crashed through his body.

There beside the ring were Rick's designer trainers.

Taz looked around wildly for any sign of Rick, but he was nowhere to be seen. Taz scanned the ground – and then he saw it.

Not far from Rick's things, resting against the base of one of the steel railings, was Rick's Zed 5. Its casing was glowing.

Taz leant over carefully to look at the screen of the Zed 5. When he saw the display, he put his hand over his mouth and felt his knees go weak.

There on the screen he could see an image of Rick falling backwards into a black abyss. Taz could just about hear Rick's voice. He was screaming, "HELP ME!"

Taz stared in shock, as Rick fell further and further away. Taz was frozen with fear and unable to move. Within seconds, Rick was just a tiny dot on the screen.

And then he completely disappeared.